To my son,
Everything beautiful in my life begins with you.

You're perfect, you're kind, you're smart,
you're intelligent. Most importantly, you're mine.
There is nothing I would change about you.

The one that loves you the most,

Mama

I am Malachi!

My mother calls me Chi.

My father calls me his little man.

My Aunts, Uncles and cousins all call me Chi Chi!

Except for my Auntie Kat, she calls me "Tete's Avatar".

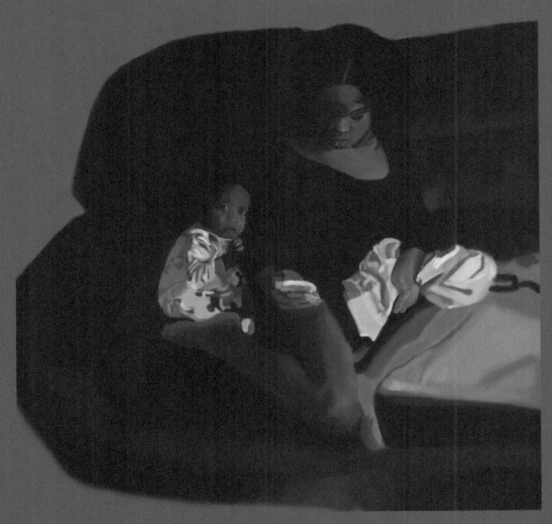

And my Uncle Sam, who calls me "Dieu".

I am Malachi, but

Some people call me Autistic, weird, loud, and "different".

Mama calls me perfect, handsome face, sweetie pie, suga, sweet love, Chi bear, amazing, brilliant..........

and intelligent.

Some of my friends call me by grabbing my hands,
touching my face, or tapping me on the shoulder.

Sometimes we stand in front of each other
in total silence......

When I visit my daddy, my Nana Lina calls me JR.

Mommy doesn't like that name much.

I visit my other Nana Mimi all the time, and she calls me boo boo.

I don't think mommy likes that name either.

My Pop Pop calls me
"Ma lonbrit"(Ma belly button), everyone
thinks it's funny.

My Pop Pop is very funny, everyone says so.

As you can see, different people call me different names.

When people ask me who I am, I proudly say.....

I am Malachi!

CPSIA information can be obtained
at www.ICGtesting.com
Printed in the USA
BVHW060348040821
613540BV00004B/118